Clitophon

A Modern Translation

Adapted for the Contemporary Reader

Plato

Translated by Tim Zengerink

Table of Contents

Preface - Message to the Reader

What If You Could Help Rebuild the Greatest Library in Human History?

Thousands of years ago, the Library of Alexandria stood as the crown jewel of human achievement — a sanctuary where the collected wisdom of every known civilization was gathered, preserved, and shared freely.

And then, it was lost.

Through fire, conquest, and the slow erosion of time, humanity lost not just books — but ideas, dreams, discoveries, and stories that could have changed the world forever.

Today, the Library of Alexandria lives again — and you are invited to be a part of its restoration.

Our mission is simple yet profound:

To rebuild the greatest library the world has ever known, and to translate all timeless works into every language and dialect, so that no seeker of knowledge is ever left behind again.

By joining our movement to rebuild the modern Library of Alexandria, you become part of an unprecedented mission:

- **Unlimited Access to the Greatest Audiobooks & eBooks Ever Written:**

  Instantly explore thousands of legendary works—Plato, Shakespeare, Jane Austen, Leo Tolstoy, and countless more. All instantly available to read or listen, placing a complete literary universe at your fingertips.

- **Beautiful Paperback & Deluxe Editions at Printing Cost**

  Own any title as an elegant paperback, deluxe hardcover, or stunning collectible boxset—offered to you at true printing cost, delivered straight to your door. Build your personal Library of Alexandria, crafted for beauty, built for durability, and worthy of proud display.

- **Fresh Translations for Modern Readers—in Every Language & Dialect**

  Enjoy timeless masterpieces reimagined in clear, contemporary language—no more outdated phrases or obscure references. Alongside the original versions, we're tirelessly translating these classics into every language and dialect imaginable, ensuring accessibility and understanding across cultures and generations.

- **Join a Global Renaissance of Literature & Knowledge**

  You directly support expanding our library, publishing deluxe editions at true cost, translating works into all global languages, and bringing humanity's greatest stories to people everywhere. By joining today, you're not just preserving a legacy of masterpieces; you set in motion a powerful wave of literary accessibility.

Become a Torchbearer of Knowledge.

Join us for free now at **LibraryofAlexandria.com**

Together, we will ensure that the light of human wisdom never fades again.

With gratitude and a shared love of knowledge,

The Modern Library of Alexandria Team

Visit:

www.libraryofalexandria.com

Or scan the code below:

Introduction
The Complete Plato Collection

The Life and Legacy of Plato:
A Philosopher for All Ages

Few figures in the history of philosophy command as much reverence, debate, and enduring influence as Plato. Born in Athens around 427 BCE, in the final years of the city's Golden Age, Plato lived through the collapse of Athenian democracy, the trial and execution of his mentor Socrates, and the rise of Macedonian power under Philip and Alexander. These tumultuous historical forces shaped his worldview, but Plato's true legacy lies in his response: not merely a political theory, but an entire philosophical vision of life, society, truth, the soul, and the cosmos.

Plato's collected works—ranging from short dialogues and letters to epic treatises like the Republic and Laws—compose one of the most complete, systematic, and expansive bodies of thought produced by any individual in the Western canon. Yet they are not mere theoretical discourses. Each dialogue is also a literary drama, a carefully crafted philosophical stage play in which characters confront questions of justice, virtue, love, death, knowledge, and reality itself. These works do not only instruct; they provoke, challenge, and awaken.

Plato's writing is unique in that it almost never speaks directly in his own voice. Instead, he channels his ideas through characters, most famously Socrates, whose sharp wit and relentless questioning became the template for philosophical inquiry itself. But while Socrates is the hero of many dialogues, Plato's vision eventually extends far beyond the life and death of his teacher. Across dozens of works, Plato constructs a philosophical edifice that has shaped metaphysics, ethics, politics, epistemology, psychology, theology, cosmology, and aesthetics for more than two thousand years.

This complete collection brings together every extant work attributed to Plato, allowing readers to follow the evolution of his thought from youthful irony to mature system-building. It includes not only the major dialogues but also the so-called apocryphal letters and later compositions like the Epinomis, providing a comprehensive view of the Platonic tradition in its historical, spiritual, and intellectual richness.

To read Plato in full is to embark on a journey through the deepest questions of human existence. This collection is more than a set of ancient texts; it is a map of the soul, a blueprint of the ideal city, a theory of reality, and a spiritual invitation to a life of inquiry, discipline, and wonder.

The Dialogues: Stages of Philosophical Development

Plato's dialogues are typically divided into three periods—early, middle, and late—each corresponding to different phases in his philosophical development. While these categories are not always precise, they help us trace Plato's intellectual evolution and appreciate the richness and diversity of his thought.

The early dialogues are often referred to as "Socratic" because they primarily serve to portray the life and method of Socrates. These include works like Euthyphro, Apology, Crito, and Protagoras. In them, Socrates emerges as the gadfly of Athens, questioning religious orthodoxy, political complacency, and ethical superficiality. The early dialogues typically end in aporia—a state of puzzlement—reflecting Socrates' belief that wisdom begins with the acknowledgment of one's ignorance. These texts are sharp, brief, and dialectical, offering little in the way of doctrine but much in the way of provocation. They invite the reader to ask: What is virtue? Can it be taught? Is piety a matter of law or reason? How should one live?

The middle dialogues mark a turning point. Here, Plato begins to develop and articulate his own philosophical doctrines, most notably the theory of Forms. Works such as Phaedo, Symposium, Republic, and Phaedrus introduce a new metaphysical and ethical framework in which reality is divided between the visible world of change and the intelligible world of eternal truths. The Forms—perfect, immaterial templates of concepts like Justice, Beauty, and Goodness—become the foundation of Plato's ontology. The Republic in particular stands as Plato's magnum opus, a comprehensive vision of a just society rooted in the tripartite nature of the soul and governed by philosopher-kings. The middle dialogues are characterized by grandeur and idealism, but they also contain some of the most poetic and mythic elements of Plato's writing. The Allegory of the Cave, the Myth of the Charioteer, and the Ladder of Love are not just illustrations—they are spiritual parables that convey profound truths about the soul's ascent from ignorance to knowledge, from appearance to reality.

In the late dialogues, Plato's tone becomes more analytical and self-critical. Works like Theaetetus, Sophist, Statesman, Philebus, and Laws exhibit a more refined and technical method, often engaging in deep metaphysical distinctions and exploring the limitations of earlier ideas. In Theaetetus, for instance, Plato reexamines the nature of knowledge, while Sophist and Parmenides critique and revise the theory of Forms itself. The Laws, Plato's longest work, lays out a practical legal code for a second-best city, acknowledging that the philosopher-king is unlikely to rule in the real world. Instead of utopia, Plato gives us a religious and educational framework for civic life—one guided by virtue, ritual, and divine order.

These dialogues demonstrate Plato's lifelong commitment to dialectic—not merely as a method, but as a way of being. They reflect a mature philosopher grappling with the limits of reason, the persistence of error, and the complexity of the human condition. By the end of his career, Plato remains faithful to the pursuit of wisdom but less certain of simple answers. His later works combine intellectual rigor with theological depth, opening new pathways for mysticism, political theory, and metaphysical speculation.

Together, the dialogues form a dramatic and philosophical epic. They invite readers not just to study ideas, but to inhabit them—to think like philosophers, to live like seekers, and to approach life with a commitment to truth, beauty, and the Good.

Plato's Enduring Influence and the Meaning of the Collection

To compile and read The Complete Plato Collection is to encounter one of the foundational pillars of Western civilization. Plato's impact spans continents, centuries, and disciplines. He was revered in antiquity, reinterpreted by Christian theologians, adopted by Islamic philosophers, revived by Renaissance humanists, and critiqued by modern thinkers from Nietzsche to Heidegger. In every age, Plato has sparked both admiration and opposition—not because he offers easy solutions, but because he dares to ask the most difficult and enduring questions.

Plato's influence can be traced in nearly every field of human thought. In politics, his vision of the philosopher-king and the well-ordered city continues to shape debates about justice, governance, and the role of intellectuals. In metaphysics, his distinction between the world of appearance and the world of Forms laid the groundwork for idealist and dualist traditions. In epistemology, his emphasis on recollection, dialectic, and the intelligible realm anticipates the structure of rational inquiry. In ethics, his exploration of virtue, the soul, and the good life remains a cornerstone of philosophical and spiritual practice.

But perhaps Plato's greatest legacy is his vision of education—not as the accumulation of facts, but as the transformation of the soul. For Plato, to learn is to turn one's whole being toward the light of truth. The dialogues are not simply arguments; they are initiations, designed to awaken in the reader a longing for wisdom and a recognition of their own inner potential. Plato's Academy, the first institution of higher learning in the Western world, embodied this ideal. It was not a place of indoctrination, but of inquiry—a community of seekers dedicated to the eternal questions.

Reading this complete collection allows one to experience the full arc of Plato's thought—from the ironic youth in search of virtue, to the system-building philosopher envisioning the ideal state, to the mystical elder contemplating the cosmos and the divine. It is a journey through one of the most powerful minds in history, and one that rewards careful, repeated, and reverent engagement.

This edition also includes lesser-known texts, epistles, and apocryphal works that, while sometimes debated in terms of authenticity, provide valuable context for understanding how Plato was remembered, interpreted, and mythologized by his followers. These texts reveal the depth of the Platonic tradition—a tradition that extended far beyond Plato himself and became the foundation for entire schools of philosophy, including Neoplatonism, which infused Platonic ideas with religious and metaphysical intensity.

Whether you are a first-time reader or a seasoned scholar, The Complete Plato Collection offers an unparalleled opportunity. It is not merely a literary or intellectual experience—it is an invitation to think more deeply, live more wisely, and participate in a tradition that stretches across the centuries. The questions Plato raised are still our questions. What is justice? What is love? What is the soul? How should we live?

This collection will not give you all the answers. But it will show you how to ask the right questions—and how to keep asking them. In doing so, it may lead you, as it led Plato, to the threshold of the eternal.

Foreword

Philosophy Interrupted: Socratic Method, Political Frustration, and the Crisis of Moral Guidance

Among Plato's many dialogues, Clitophon stands out as one of the most curious and controversial. Brief, abrupt, and structurally unconventional, the dialogue consists almost entirely of a monologue by the character Clitophon, directed at Socrates, criticizing him for failing to offer substantive moral guidance beyond motivational rhetoric. Unlike the sustained dialectical exchanges seen in most Platonic dialogues, Clitophon reads more like a philosophical outburst—one that raises more questions than it answers and leaves readers with a sense of unresolved tension. This has led to centuries of debate regarding its purpose, authenticity, and placement within Plato's body of work.

Despite—or perhaps because of—its brevity and incompleteness, Clitophon is a powerful exploration of the limits of philosophical exhortation. It highlights the potential gap between the inspirational role of the philosopher and the actual instruction needed for the pursuit of justice and virtue. It challenges not only the adequacy of Socratic method but the reader's own expectations of philosophy. What good is motivation if it lacks method? What use is questioning if it leads only to uncertainty? And at what point does philosophy need to move from critique to construction?

The central figure, Clitophon, is not one of Plato's major characters. He appears briefly elsewhere in Republic as a minor political figure, aligned with the democratic faction. Here, he takes center stage and delivers a pointed critique of Socrates, whom he once admired. Clitophon praises Socrates for awakening a desire for justice in his listeners but accuses him of failing to articulate what justice actually is or how one might acquire it. He claims that Socrates excels at refuting false beliefs and rousing souls toward the good, but never crosses the threshold into positive teaching. The result, he argues, is that Socrates leaves his followers in a state of yearning without guidance.

This criticism is profound. It touches on the very essence of the Socratic method—its emphasis on questioning rather than teaching, on intellectual humility rather than doctrinal certainty. It also mirrors historical tensions between philosophy and politics, between contemplation and action, and between inspiration and instruction. In this way, Clitophon functions not only as a critique of Socrates but as a self-reflection on philosophy itself. It is Plato's most direct confrontation with the potential shortcomings of his own master's legacy.

In this introduction, we will examine Clitophon across three major dimensions. First, we will consider the historical and dramatic context of the dialogue, exploring Clitophon's political background, the ambiguity of the text's authorship, and its possible relationship to Republic. Second, we will analyze the philosophical content of Clitophon's speech, focusing on his critique of Socrates, his demand for practical ethics, and the broader implications for philosophical education. Finally, we will reflect on the significance of Clitophon in the Platonic corpus, considering whether it represents a critique from within or outside Plato's own philosophy, and what it reveals about the challenges of turning moral insight into action. In doing so, we will see that this brief and unusual text raises some of the deepest questions in all of Platonic thought—questions that remain vital to our understanding of justice, virtue, and the role of philosophy in everyday life.

A Dialogue Without Dialogue:
Dramatic Context and Interpretive

Challenges

The first striking feature of Clitophon is its unusual structure. While most of Plato's dialogues unfold through a back-and-forth of philosophical questioning, Clitophon is dominated almost entirely by a monologue. After a few brief lines of exchange, Clitophon launches into an extended critique of Socrates, recounting their past interactions and explaining his frustrations. Socrates himself remains silent throughout, leaving the reader to imagine what his response might have been— or whether the critique stands unanswered.

This lack of balance has led to speculation about the dialogue's authorship. Some ancient commentators questioned whether Plato wrote it at all, and modern scholars remain divided. Its style is more direct and rhetorical than Plato's typical work, and it lacks the dramatic subtlety and narrative polish found in Republic, Phaedrus, or Symposium. Yet there are strong reasons to consider Clitophon authentically Platonic. It engages with core themes of Platonic philosophy, mirrors debates present in other dialogues, and may serve as a bridge or preface to larger works— particularly Republic.

One popular theory is that Clitophon was originally intended as an introduction to Republic, explaining why

Clitophon does not participate in the larger conversation. Indeed, Republic opens with Socrates encountering Polemarchus and others, with Clitophon present but silent. If so, Clitophon serves as both a dramatic and philosophical prelude, illustrating the urgency and confusion that Socrates' interlocutors feel before launching into the full-scale inquiry into justice and the ideal city.

Clitophon himself is an intriguing figure. In historical Athens, he was known as a moderate democrat, often advocating for political compromise. His philosophical persona reflects this disposition—he is caught between admiration for Socrates and impatience with his methods. He wants answers, not just questions. He seeks knowledge that can be applied to political life, not merely contemplation that remains private and inconclusive. His critique is thus rooted not in hostility, but in disappointment. He expected more from philosophy—and he is not sure it has delivered.

This background gives the dialogue its emotional weight. It is not a playful or hypothetical exchange. It is a serious charge made by a serious man against a revered thinker. Whether or not Plato agreed with Clitophon's critique, he took it seriously enough to preserve and dramatize it. And in doing so, he invites us to do the same.

The Critique of Socrates:
From Exhortation to Instruction

Clitophon begins his speech by expressing gratitude to Socrates for awakening his concern for justice. He recounts how Socrates inspired him to reject wealth, power, and bodily pleasure in favor of virtue and the soul's well-being. Through his analogies, public speeches, and refutations, Socrates made Clitophon—and many others—feel that the pursuit of justice was the most important task in life. But, Clitophon says, that is where Socrates stops. He excels at convincing people that they need to care about justice, but he offers no clear account of what justice is or how to become just.

This complaint hinges on the distinction between protreptic and didactic philosophy. Protreptic philosophy exhorts—it encourages, inspires, and motivates. Didactic philosophy teaches—it explains, demonstrates, and instructs. Clitophon accuses Socrates of being exclusively protreptic. He is like a doctor who tells a patient to pursue health but offers no diagnosis or prescription. Or like a trainer who tells someone to exercise but provides no regimen.

This analogy is more than rhetorical. It cuts to the heart of Socratic method. Socrates famously claimed not to possess knowledge, only to help others discover it through questioning. He insisted on starting with ignorance, exposing contradictions in others' beliefs, and refraining from asserting positive doctrines. Clitophon finds this frustrating. He wants Socrates to move from critique to construction, from refutation to instruction. In his view, knowing that one should pursue justice is not enough—one must also know what justice is and how to embody it.

Clitophon tries to extract an answer from Socrates. He proposes that justice might be helping friends and harming enemies, or minding one's own business, or benefiting others. But each time, Socrates refutes the suggestion, showing that these definitions are either too vague or lead to contradictions. For Clitophon, this is not progress—it is evasion. He suspects that Socrates is more interested in questioning than in answering, in appearing wise than in teaching wisdom.

Yet even as Clitophon criticizes Socrates, he acknowledges the power of his method. Socrates has accomplished something remarkable: he has shaken people from complacency, ignited a passion for virtue, and created a sense of urgency about the moral life. This, in itself, is no small achievement. But Clitophon's question is whether this is enough. Can philosophy fulfill its mission if it inspires without instructing? Can it guide the city if it refuses to offer clear principles?

And can it shape the soul if it never defines what the good truly is?

These questions remain unanswered in the dialogue. Socrates says nothing. Clitophon leaves the stage still searching, still uncertain. The reader is left to decide whether his critique is fair, whether Socrates' silence is damning or instructive, and whether the philosophical path must eventually lead from inquiry to doctrine.

Philosophy and Its Limits: Instruction, Virtue, and the Political Life

The tension dramatized in Clitophon lies at the heart of Plato's broader philosophical project. It is the tension between knowing and doing, between motivating and educating, between private reflection and public action. Clitophon wants philosophy to do more—to guide the soul, shape the city, and clarify the path to justice. Socrates, by contrast, seems content to question, to expose, and to wait for wisdom to emerge through dialogue.

In later dialogues, Plato attempts to bridge this gap. In Republic, Socrates constructs an elaborate theory of justice, virtue, and the ideal state. In Laws, Plato designs a complete legal system, filled with moral instruction and civic rituals. In Phaedrus and Symposium, he explores the role of love and inspiration in the soul's ascent to truth. But these later works do not contradict Clitophon—they respond to it. They build upon the questions raised here and attempt to answer them more fully.

Yet Plato never abandons the Socratic insight that knowledge begins in ignorance and that the love of wisdom is a journey, not a destination. Even in Republic, the final vision of the Good remains elusive, beyond description. Even in Laws, the laws themselves are tools for soul-shaping, not ends in themselves. The critique posed in Clitophon is not rejected—it is absorbed and transformed.

For modern readers, Clitophon remains a mirror. It reflects our desire for certainty, guidance, and instruction in a world full of confusion and contradiction. It challenges us to consider whether philosophy must provide answers or whether its truest function is to awaken the soul. It forces us to ask whether moral education requires rules or reflection, and whether the highest form of wisdom is found in the journey or the destination.

The genius of Clitophon lies in its unresolved nature. It ends not with a triumph of reason or a revelation of truth, but with an impasse. It captures a moment of philosophical crisis—a turning point where admiration turns to frustration, where inquiry threatens to dissolve into skepticism, and where the need for justice becomes a demand for direction.

In the final analysis, Clitophon is not an attack on philosophy—it is an invitation to deepen it. It challenges philosophers to move beyond critique, to strive for clarity, and to connect their insights to the real needs of the soul and the city. It reminds us that the love of wisdom is not only about questioning others, but about questioning oneself. And it shows that even the harshest criticisms of Socrates can lead not away from philosophy, but deeper into its heart.

Clitophon

SOCRATES: Someone recently told me that Clitophon, son of Aristonymus, has been talking with Lysias and criticizing those who spend time with me. He said you strongly praised time spent with Thrasymachus instead.

CLITOPHON: Whoever said that didn't explain the conversation accurately, Socrates. It's true that I didn't praise everything about you—but I didn't criticize everything either. And since you seem upset, even though you're acting like you don't care, I'm happy to explain everything I said, especially since we're alone right now. Maybe you heard it wrong, and you've judged me too harshly. If you'll allow me to speak freely, I'll gladly explain myself.

SOCRATES: Of course I'll listen. It would be wrong not to, especially if it could help me improve. If I find out what I do well and what I don't, I can try to do better.

CLITOPHON: Then here's what I said. When I'm with you, Socrates, I often find myself amazed by what you say. Compared to most people, you speak beautifully, especially when you correct others. You

23

sound almost like a voice from the heavens when you say things like:

"Where are you all rushing off to? Don't you realize you're doing everything wrong? You care so much about making money but ignore your own children— children who will inherit that money but don't know how to use it properly. You don't even look for teachers to help them learn justice—if it can be taught—or to help them train in it, if it takes practice. You also don't take care of yourselves. You and your kids may have studied reading, music, and sports, but clearly you're no better off morally than others who haven't. So why do you still follow the same weak education system instead of looking for people who can help you live better lives?"

You go on to say that wars, arguments, and injustice happen not because someone misses a beat in music or dance, but because of people who live without purpose or values. You challenge the belief that people are unjust by choice and argue that no one would choose something so harmful on purpose. People say they do wrong because they're overcome by pleasure, but doesn't that mean it's not a choice, but something forced on them?

You explain that unjust actions are actually done unwillingly—and this means that individuals and entire cities need to take their actions more seriously.

When I hear these kinds of things from you, Socrates, I admire you deeply. You make such strong, inspiring arguments. I've often told others how powerful and moving your words are. I also agree with you when you say that people who train their bodies but ignore their souls are doing things backwards—they focus on what should be ruled (the body), instead of what should rule (the soul). And you say that someone who doesn't know how to use their soul should not be living freely, because they'll only harm themselves or others. That person should either not live at all or live under the guidance of someone wiser—just like a ship should be steered by someone trained in navigation. You call that skill the "art of politics," and you say it's the same as the art of justice.

When you speak like this, Socrates, I never object. I truly believe what you say is important, powerful, and eye-opening. It's like waking up from a deep sleep. I've taken your advice to heart, and I've been eager to hear what comes next.

So I started asking your close friends and students—those who are always around you—what we're supposed to do after accepting your teachings. I asked them:

"What are we supposed to do now? Are we just going to keep giving inspiring speeches to people who haven't been inspired yet? And after we've all been inspired, then what? Don't we need to figure out how to begin living justly?"

It's like if someone told us to take care of our bodies, and then criticized us for focusing too much on food and drink instead of learning how to stay healthy. We would ask what art or knowledge teaches this— gymnastics or medicine? And if someone told us to take care of our souls, we'd ask: What is the art that teaches us justice?

One of your students told me that the art we were looking for was justice itself. So I asked, "Don't just give me the name. What does this art actually do?" Like medicine produces health, and carpentry produces furniture, what does justice produce?

Some said it's "what's appropriate," "what fits," "what's useful," or "what benefits others." But I pointed out that all arts aim at these things, yet each has a clear goal—medicine aims at health, carpentry at good furniture. So what is the actual result of justice?

Finally, one of your companions said that the true work of justice is creating friendship among citizens. But when we asked whether friendship is always good, he said yes. Then we asked whether even the friendships of wild animals and kids counted—since those are often harmful. He said no, only true friendship is good, and that true friendship is agreement based on knowledge, not just opinion. But then we ran into trouble. If justice is agreement in knowledge, then what separates it from all the other arts? All of them involve agreement and knowledge. And yet, we couldn't figure out what justice actually does—what its specific work is.

Eventually, I came to ask you the same thing. You told me that justice is helping your friends and harming your enemies. But then you changed your mind and said a just person never harms anyone—they only help.

I've gone through this cycle with you more than once, Socrates. I've tried to get clear answers from you. I think you're the best person at encouraging people to care about virtue—but I also think you stop there. Either you don't know what justice really is, or you won't share it with me. That's why I've decided to go to Thrasymachus and others who might help me finally get answers.

I wouldn't be doing this if you had continued your guidance. For example, if someone gave a speech encouraging me to take care of my body, they'd also explain what my body needs. In the same way, you've convinced me to take care of my soul—but now I want you to show me what it needs.

So imagine I'm saying, "You're right, Socrates—it's foolish to care about everything except the soul, which is the most important." Please tell me what comes next. If you don't, I'll end up doing what I've already done: praising you to others, but also criticizing you for not helping us go further.

You're incredibly valuable to someone who hasn't been inspired yet. But for someone who's ready to live a good life, you might actually hold them back from reaching it.

The End

Thank You for Reading

Dear Reader,

We hope this timeless classic has sparked your imagination and enriched your literary journey. Now that you've turned the final page, we want to share a vision for the future of reading—one where every classic you've ever wanted to explore is at your fingertips, in a format that best suits your life.

We'd like to invite you to gain immediate, unlimited digital & audiobook access to hundreds of the most treasured literary classics ever written—along with the option to secure deluxe paperback, hardcover & box set editions at printing cost. Together, we can spark a new global literary renaissance alongside our small, independent publishing house called "The Library of Alexandria."

Thousands of years ago, the Library of Alexandria stood as a beacon of knowledge—until it was lost to history. We aim to reignite that spirit of preservation and discovery right now, in the modern age—only this time, it's accessible to all, in every language and every format.

Picture a world where every timeless classic, novel, poem, or philosophical treatise is not only available to read but also updated for today's readers—modernized, translated into any language or dialect, and ready to enjoy in any format you choose, whether that is in an eBook, audiobook, paperback, or deluxe hardcover & box set version a printing cost.

By joining our movement to rebuild the modern Library of Alexandria, you become part of an unprecedented mission to offer:

- **Unlimited Audiobook & eBook Access to the Greatest Classics of All Time**

  Instantly explore thousands of legendary works, from Plato and Shakespeare to Jane Austen and Leo Tolstoy. All are instantly ready to read or listen to, giving you a complete literary universe at your fingertips.

- **Paperback & Deluxe Editions at Printing Costs:**

  Purchase any title in a paperback, deluxe hardbound, or deluxe boxset edition at printing costs, shipped right to your doorstep. Curate your personal library of Alexandria with editions worthy of display— crafted to last, designed to captivate, and delivered straight to your door.

- **Modern translations for Contemporary Readers in all languages and dialects**

  Discover a vast selection of classics reimagined in clear, current language—no more struggling with outdated phrases or obscure references. Next to the original versions, we aim to offer translations in as many languages and dialects as possible.

  As we continue our translation efforts and add new languages, readers everywhere can connect with these works as if they were written today. By bridging linguistic divides, you're contributing to ensuring that these timeless stories become more meaningful, accessible, and inspiring for people across the globe.

- **Your Personal Library of Alexandria:**

  Over the months and years, you'll curate a unique physical archive of classics—each volume a testament to your taste, curiosity, and love of knowledge. It's not just about owning books—it's about curating a cultural legacy you'll cherish and pass down for generations to come.

- **Join a Global Literary Renaissance:**

  Your support fuels an ongoing mission: allowing us to reinvest in offering deluxe print editions (including special boxsets) at their true cost, broaden the range of available formats and translations, and extend the reach of these works to new audiences worldwide. By joining today, you're not just preserving a legacy of masterpieces; you set in motion a powerful wave of literary accessibility.

We are more than a publisher—we're a movement, and we can't do it alone. Your support lets us scale our mission, preserving and reimagining history's greatest works for tomorrow's readers.

Become a Torchbearer of knowledge.

Thank you for picking up this book and allowing us into your literary journey. As you turn the pages, know that you're part of something larger: a global effort to keep these stories alive, share their wisdom across borders and generations, and spark a true cultural revival for the modern era.

If this resonates with you—please consider taking the next step by visiting:

www.libraryofalexandria.com

With gratitude and a shared love of knowledge,

The Modern Library of Alexandria Team

Visit:

www.libraryofalexandria.com

Or scan the code below: